AMERICAN FLOATERS

seven short stories for young adults

JOHN NAPOLITANO

American Floaters

For information, address Sandlot Books, P.O. Box 420, La Harpe, IL 61450.

Printed in the United States of America.

ISBN: 0-9768877-0-3

Library of Congress Control Number: 2005904794

for Bridget and Luke

Contents

1. Lance Erger 11

2. The Force of Gravity 33

3. Last-Minute Shopping 50

4. Blamemaster 2000 69

5. Hard Sell 90

6. Kite Day 111

7. The Course of Empire 134

Acknowledgments

My gratitude extends to those individuals who helped with the production of this book. First to my wife Bridget, frontline editor and continual source of encouragement, and my son Luke whose keen eyes have taught me how to find much more in life. For generously giving of their time and expertise, I'd also like to thank Lisa Bywaters, Dr. David Stevenson, Christina McCaslin, and Aaron and Linda Baker—I'm indebted to each one of you.

AMERICAN FLOATERS

LANCE ERGER

Only a week ago Lenny Berger III was a nobody. He didn't have any friends, and no one even looked at him. As he fumbled down the hallways of Metro Consolidated High School, he was like a discarded foam cup, spiraling over the highway, passing under cars, buses, and heavily-laden semi trucks. If he had suddenly disappeared or been crushed by a surge of foot traffic, none of the students would have noticed. Not even the teachers, who rarely acknowledged him anyway, and when they did, merely pointed in his general direction and mumbled. Perhaps only Mr. Mattox the janitor would have briefly noted his flattened body before sweeping it into a dustpan filled with crumpled notes, candy wrappers, and chewed pen caps. (Lenny figured it must be the same for all skinny kids with pimples, weak chins, crooked teeth, and bad names.)

Each new day was the same day for Lenny. He went to school, he came home, he watched television. . . . Went to school, came home, watched television. . . . School, home, television.

Because Mr. and Mrs. Berger worked late and often vacationed overseas, they bought their son a 50" Maximizer Platinum Series television, which Lenny eventually nicknamed "Max." Lenny never turned the television off. Instead, he let Max fill the house with brilliant images, a colorful kaleidoscope of game shows, talk shows, cartoons, infomercials, dubbed kung-fu epics, news, African safaris, made-for-television movies, music videos, cooking seminars, and even an amateur Siberian channel devoted to the preservation of traditional reindeer milking.

Lenny would recline himself on the couch in front of Max, bury his right hand in a bag of potato chips, and palm the television remote in his left. He'd speak out loud as he jumped from station to station, exercising the full range of satellite programming. With picture-in-picture, he could easily layer several channels, and the end effect was similar to a choppy dream, a flashing, two-dimensional landscape that took him through time and across entire continents.

In the course of one afternoon, Max brought Lenny through deep space and equally far into human anatomy, the setting for many public television specials about living tissue and organ transplants. Max brought Lenny to the top of Mt. Everest on the back of a stout sherpa named Ebu while simultaneously diving for buried treasure in shark-infested water off the coast of Australia.

Lenny had driven behind the wheel of a stock car, battled alien invaders, harvested wheat in Nebraska, parachuted from an airplane, gone undercover with CIA operatives, and learned how to properly wire an electrical outlet. He could prepare a Thanksgiving turkey and knew how to start and manage a vineyard.

On average, Lenny spent 10 hours watching television every day during the week. On Saturday and Sunday, he logged about 24, which brought his weekly total to roughly 74 hours of intense, concentrated viewing. As a result, it wasn't long before Lenny became a kind of television authority. He knew every station like hues on a painter's palette and could navigate his way to find the most remote subject matter within seconds. For instance, with only a few deft movements of his thumb, he could locate an image of magnified toe fungus or rare black and white movies of Elvis curling spaghetti onto a fork—he was that good.

And he didn't need a television guide because he already knew where to look. Lenny spent so much time with Max that he eventually heard the mysterious language of television waves that hummed beneath the channel numbers and satellite positions. He no longer relied on complex menus and viewing schedules but instead looked beyond the screen and deep into the signal, which seemed to invite him in like a good friend.

One day in the middle of September, Lenny's life changed forever. He was peddling his bike over Main Street and watching the portable television that his mother had mailed from Japan, when he rode over a broken beer bottle. In what seemed like Hollywood slow motion, the sharp edges burst his front tire and caused him to pitch sideways over the handlebars.

Before he could raise his head off the pavement, Lenny heard screeching tires and looked up into a chrome grill. He didn't move, only fixed his gaze on a twitching bug caught in the radiator.

"Are you okay," a woman's voice sounded above him. "Here let me help you. Thank goodness you're all right. But your arms. We'll need to get some bandages on your hands and your arms."

Lenny recognized the woman. She was the school counselor, Ms. White, an energetic woman with a thin line of dark hair above her upper lip. She had called him into her office several times during "Be a Friend Week" to give him peppermint candies and stickers.

"Hey, I know you. Lance, right? Lance Erger."

Lenny nodded without thinking. He dusted his knees and told her that he would be fine. *Lance*, he thought, *Lance Erger*. He liked the sound of that.

"You're one tough kid," she said, patting his shoulder. "Maybe you'll be a stuntman someday."

"Oh, it's nothing. Do it all the time," Lenny said

and began to feel a new energy come over him.

He looked now at all the people who had gathered around. They anticipated something. They looked in awe, and that made him squint and flare his nostrils. They grouped in clusters on the sidewalk and slowed their cars to get a better look at him. Lenny just slouched and hooked his right thumb into the pocket of his jeans.

Lance.

"I really should get you to a hospital, so they can check you out. Just in case. You're bleeding."

Lenny made a long, concentrated inspection of Ms. White and, for some strange reason, thought about smoking a cigarette. He had never smoked one before but wanted to now, the way they do on television and then confidently flick the butt against the windshield of her car. But he didn't have any cigarettes, so he unwrapped a stick of sugarless bubble gum and let the paper fall to the street.

As Lenny chewed, he scanned the faces around him and stopped at a cute girl standing with her boyfriend. He gave her a wink and, without speaking, picked up his bike and walked it back across the street. The front tire wobbled and squeaked.

Lance.

Traffic had stopped now. Children hung out of windows and pointed. Several women with curlers in their hair stood in a doorway. A tall woman jogged in place next to a stop sign. A brown-clothed delivery man held a clipboard to his brow like a sun visor. They were all looking at him. They were looking at Lenny now. Many had seen the whole incident, the way he cleared the handlebars of his bike and came down onto the pavement. They had also seen the car skid to a stop inches from his unblinking face and the way he casually stood and spoke to the woman. And the way he chewed his gum, lips parted and askew.

Now they watched him limp across the street

with lines of blood running down his right cheek. Lenny felt their heavy gaze and knew they wanted him to stay. But he ignored them, just limped and snapped his gum before he disappeared from view down an alley.

Lance.

Behind him, a little boy in a wagon pointed his finger at the sun and mouthed an inaudible word. Then everyone slowly returned to what they had been doing. Some shook their heads. Others dialed cell phones and spoke quickly with arm movements, describing what they had seen.

Ms. White looked down and touched the front of her car. Then, dazed, she drove away.

Lenny ate macaroni and cheese from a plastic container that night. He stared at the television screen. They were airing a rerun of his favorite program, *Mobster's Five*, the one about Sammy "The Lobster" Milano and Googa "Two Guns" the peanut vender.

At 7:12, Lenny sighed and thought. He went into his closet and took out the black suit that his mother made him wear to funerals. He put it on and stood in the bathroom. He got up close to the mirror and said the word "Lance." He said it slowly and then pointed to himself. "Lance." He touched his lips, snarled, wrinkled his forehead, and spit into the sink. He said it again. This time, he messed up his hair and pulled off the bandage above his left eye. Then he smirked. "I guess you're the one who's been fooled, Two Guns," he said roughly, tossing out the words. He shrugged his shoulders and swept his hand through the air. "This is Milano territory. It will *always* be Milano territory."

News about Lance spread quickly. Everyone wanted to see the new student. They came out of classrooms pointing.

"Yea, that's the guy who was hit by a car yesterday. I saw the whole thing. Then he just got up and walked away."

"My father says he's some kind of teenage superhero or a Secret Service agent."

"What's his name?"

"Get this, his name is Lance Erger."

"Man, he *must* be cool."

"Probably from New York."

"I think he's foreign, maybe from Europe or Italy."

"Think he'd come to your party Friday?"

Lenny heard the whispers but didn't say anything, only walked with a subtle limp and stared at the floor. After opening his locker, he made one poised movement and removed his digital wristwatch. He checked the time, tucked his math book under one arm, and slammed his locker door shut.

The hallway became silent.

Lenny turned around and adjusted the sleeves of his suit coat while violently sucking air between his two front teeth.

A pretty, dark-haired girl, standing only a few feet away, passed out at the sight, and Lenny whirled around and caught her in midair, careful to cradle her neck against his forearm. Everyone gasped and then sighed when he slid his coat off, placed it under her head, and casually walked to class where he sat in the back row and looked over his dark sunglasses.

The next period was English, and he read a poem hastily composed on the back of a napkin.

In science he wrote secret notes, unintelligible riddles that he passed to a few students.

In P.E., Lenny discovered that he could juggle basketballs.

At lunch, he sat alone, at the far end of the cafeteria, peeling an orange. Lenny watched his hands as they removed the peel in a single sinuous curl. They were different now, not his own. When people looked at him, he made biting gestures in the air.

Throughout the afternoon, students began to follow him. They did everything he did. Lenny'd slam his locker—they'd slam their lockers. He'd stop for a drink—they'd drink. He'd spit—they'd spit. Some had even begun to limp. But no one spoke to him. They stayed back a few feet or rushed ahead to open doors.

When the bell rang at the end of the day, Lenny raised his hands over his head and, like a primitive warrior, screamed his way down the hall and out the front doors of the school.

The pretty girl, who now donned his suit coat, stood with a crowd of students gathering to watch his erratic movements over the football field. She brought one of the sleeves to her nose and drew a concentrated breath. Then everyone came close to her and touched the fabric. They put their hands inside the pockets and found funeral programs and sugarless gum, which they returned with slow, reverent movements before dispersing quietly.

The next day, several students wore suit coats

to school, old ones, hand-me-downs. Dark, thick-rimmed glasses were everywhere, and most of the school had acquired a slight limp. They slammed their lockers. The captain of the football team had even thrown himself off a bike, proudly wearing the scrapes and bruises like an initiation patch. Everyone milled about in the hallway and exchanged secret notes. They wanted to see Lance. They wanted to be near him.

"There he is!" someone yelled, and a mob rushed to the front doors but was disappointed to find a freshman look-alike with an orange.

They pressed themselves up against the windows and stared into the parking lot. But Lance didn't show. He didn't come to school at all that day or the next. In fact, he didn't make an appearance for the rest of the week.

Every day the conversations surrounding this mysterious student intensified. Some believed that he had jumped a freight train out of town. And others were convinced that he was some kind of deep-cover agent working for a foreign government and that his mission was now complete. (The pretty girl with Lenny's suit coat began charging a nominal fee to smell and touch the fabric and brass buttons.)

But Lenny didn't go anywhere. He was at home in front of the television. What started in the street with Ms. White was becoming complete in front of Max. Lenny was slowly beginning to change and acquire new powers. He was no longer Lenny Berger III, nobody, but transforming into Lance, Lance Erger, or just "LE" (which was the way he planned to sign autographs, making the "E" larger and darker).

The more Lenny watched television, the stronger Lance became. Now, after his parents left for work, he sat with a notebook and absorbed everything. He watched it all: westerns, romance, action-adventure, comedy, only breaking to use the bathroom. He watched commercials, soap operas, sitcoms, talk shows, and more commercials. He took notes. He stayed up all night and through the next day and the next, gorging himself on the television waves and images that began to warm him. Lenny began to feel that Lance was taking control of his entire body and mind. He was gaining more and more strength, on the brink of telling him something profound, of making some monumental change inside him.

On the third day, Lance emerged from Lenny's bedroom. He wore spandex covered by a plastic shower curtain sown into baggy pants and a kind of makeshift poncho. He had Lenny's dark-rimmed glasses but had broken the lenses out and replaced them with scotch tape, which made everything blurry. On the back of his shirt, through the plastic, were the letters "LE." He wore boots from the army surplus and gauntlet biking gloves. On his head was a plastic cowboy hat from Yee-Ha Chicken Palace.

All the way to school, Lance ran up behind trees and traversed back and forth over people's yards. Occasionally, he hopped with both feet together like a cartoon bunny. Although no one could see his eyes, they darted to the side and then up. His breathing was heavy but not labored—he felt strong and hadn't even eaten breakfast or slept in days. He stood upright at the corner, chest out, arms outspread like wings. An SUV passed, and a businessman lowered his travel mug in time to see Lance Erger, flapping his arms like a steady migrating goose.

And in his mind he *was* flying. His senses were so acute that Lance could even hear voices in the telephone wires. Behind him, in the window of Get Your Cash Pawn Shop, a television showed an anchorman, deadpan, serious, the image of a fire burning above his left shoulder.

The news of Lance's return reached school before he had crossed the railroad tracks that separated town. Students grouped together, some in doorways, some by their cars in the parking lot. Other students suspected that Lance would come in a back entrance and covered the service doors and fire exits. The teachers were also smiling. They carried papers or coffee down the hallway, in their minds making excuses to look out the windows.

When Lance finally appeared, he was holding hands with a line of kindergartners, who were crossing the street to the elementary building. On the sidewalk, he waved dramatically to the kids, and with his head down, strolled into the group of high school students and teachers who had migrated out the front doors. They parted to let him pass through and extended their arms toward the crinkled plastic draped over his narrow shoulders. The pretty girl came up behind him and caught the trailing edge of his garment. Lance stopped abruptly, and the crowd became silent.

He turned slowly and spoke, "You deserve factory direct prices," he said, lowering his arm and taking her hand. "Why pay retail? 10, 20, 30—up to 50% savings, storewide! Register for a shopping spree and save! You don't want to miss this one—Friday, Saturday, and Sunday only! Order now—pay later! While supplies last!" He looked up into the air above the students, at the clouds parting, revealing blue and continued. "Many styles to choose from—everything must go! More colors and sizes! No interest, no payments for an entire year! Free t-shirt with every purchase and free shipping with orders over $50! Open a charge account and take off an additional 10%. Visit us on the web."

The students and teachers responded in a synchronous drone, their mouths agape, and then more silence. A few transcribed his words in notebooks and took pictures. Lance stood amid them, raised his voice to full crescendo, and pointed at a lone dove perched on an electrical wire.

"Looks like a mild week. Clouds and some sun. Expect rain for the big game this weekend. But should that stop us from driving our cattle? Are we going to let some big shot rancher tell us what to do? I ride the subway just like everyone else, and I don't anticipate any tomatoes. Not this year. Ground's too moist. Better plant some gourds or maybe popping corn. Hey, but we're all winners on the *Name It Game*! Just put your hand in the box and be the first to guess what name-brand product you're touching. There's money, money, money to beeeeeee won! Our first contestant is a mother of three from Tipi, California. Welcome Mary Smith. A plain name but *not* a plain toothpaste. Try it for a week, and we guarantee your brilliantly white teeth will make people like you. Are you feeling tired? Have you lost your youthful pep?

Then you need Lightning Bolt, an all-natural dietary supplement that enhances your body's cells by dispersing low-level static electricity into your bloodstream. (Side effects are generally mild and may include teeth chattering, household blackouts, and uncontrollable skipping.) Ask your doctor if Lightning Bolt is right for you. How long were you married before you found out that your husband was an alien? Because if you were injured on the job, you are entitled to compensation. Call the law firm of Messing, Messing, and Bright. We represent *YOUR* interests. 1–800–YOU–WIN2. That's 1–800–YOU–WIN2. Join us next time when we send our camera crew inside the den of a hibernating grizzly bear."

Then, as suddenly as he began, Lance stopped, letting his voice trail off and turn into pensive thought. He looked into their faces, the students and teachers. He understood how much they needed him now. They were like helpless children, small boats tossed upon the ocean without rudders. But he was going to become their wind and direction home. Lance knew that he was made to guide them and fill their sails. He would use his gift to enhance their lives and save them.

THE FORCE OF GRAVITY

Delilah Quasar was posed in her chair, knees together, legs leaning slightly to one side. She sat up straight and spoke to a friend, straining over the noise. Sam set his books down and became aware of her perfume, which was light and fresh, like a bowl of fruit rinsed under cold water and set to dry.

The fifth hour bell rang. Mr. Anderson came through the door with a stack of papers, muttering to himself.

"All right, all right. Hope you like your new seats."

The students groaned.

Sam took out his homework and a pen. Then he looked at his hands. Less than a foot away, Delilah, the most beautiful and most popular girl in school, tapped one pink fingernail on her open notebook. Fumbling to think, Sam lowered his head and noticed that her white sneakers bobbed occasionally, and he could see where her left big toe made a slight impression in the leather upper. He raised his eyes and noticed her mature figure and the thick tan sweater that gently hugged under her chin. Her dark hair fell in loose strands over her cheeks and shoulders.

Homework was called to the end of each row, and Sam passed his to the right, to Delilah, who inadvertently brushed the side of his hand. He relished the sensation that lingered and faked an overconcentrated stare at the object that Mr. Anderson now held above his head at the front of the class.

The room became silent, and Delilah wrote

something in the upper corner of her paper. For some reason, Sam did the same.

"If this tennis ball were the nucleus of a hydrogen atom, its single electron would orbit four miles away."

A few students exhaled in disbelief.

"Think about that for a moment. Four miles is roughly the distance to Gilbert's Auto Shop at the edge of town. Bet you didn't know there was that much space in an atom," Mr. Anderson said as he turned to the board and drew a nucleus with one orbiting electron.

A student in the front row raised his hand. "Last night I was thinking that atoms are a lot like our solar system. You know like the sun and the planets."

"That's a very good observation, Jason. Atoms do seem to have a similar design; however, electrons don't orbit the nucleus in predictable paths like planets. Instead, they buzz in random directions so fast that they actually create a virtually impenetrable sphere. And instead of being held in place by gravity, atoms are bound by strong and weak nuclear forces, which we are going to talk about tomorrow." Responding to the resulting blank stares, Mr. Anderson pointed to a pedestal fan in the corner. "Okay, think of it this way. That fan is off now, so it would be very easy to put your finger between the blades. But what if it were turned on? The rotating fan would create an almost solid barrier."

A football player in the back row said something under his breath, "Depends how quick you are."

The class chuckled as Mr. Anderson turned up a row and walked toward the back. "Well, Mr. Lender, what if that same fan blade were turning faster than a jet turbine? Then do you think you could *safely* stick your finger through?"

The class looked at quarterback Troy Lender,

who smirked. “Maybe not.”

“I didn’t think so. The point is, people, that there’s a lot of empty space in an atom. Yet despite all of this space the smallest speck observable under our most powerful microscope is large enough to contain 10 billion atoms. Atoms are that small.”

Sam noticed Delilah copying the diagram that Mr. Anderson had drawn on the board. She took a few notes and put a star and then a heart in the margin. As she wrote, Sam watched her long, slender fingers and her hands, the way she held her pen like a movie star. He looked up discreetly at her profile, delicate and smooth.

Someone’s stomach groaned loudly, and Delilah rolled her eyes to a friend.

Mr. Anderson turned to the class. “I realize that physics is probably the last thing on your minds before lunch, but think about this for a moment. If the laws that govern our universe’s four basic forces—gravity, electromagnetism, and strong and weak nuclear forces—were to be even slightly altered, life as we know it would cease to exist—no Friday night football games, no movies, no cars, no pizza, no rap music, no Internet—no you. So when we talk about physics, we're talking about the laws that sustain our lives. This is important stuff."

Mr. Anderson made his way back to the front of the class and wrote "GRAVITY" on the board. He underlined it twice and referred back to the tennis ball that he held up once again. "Let's review. What happens when we condense atoms together?"

A student responded, "We increase the mass."

"That's correct. And what happens when we increase the mass of an object?"

The class sat silent for a moment until a girl replied in almost a question, "It gets heavier?"

Mr. Anderson jumped slightly and pointed. "Exactly!"

A foreign exchange student in the front row flinched, and the class started laughing.

"Sorry, Francesca, I just get a little excited when it comes to gravity, which is—incidentally—the oldest force in the universe and certainly important for us here on earth because if our sun were any larger, it would exert more gravity, eventually drawing our planet into itself. At the same time, if it were not large enough, we would go careening out of our present orbit and end up freezing to death in the vacuum of deep space. Same concept could be applied to our moon. If the earth were larger, it would actually pull the moon into itself. If it were any smaller, the moon would travel out into space."

"That would make romantic strolls on the beach a bummer," someone said.

Mr. Anderson was quick to respond, "No, actually that would make them impossible because you wouldn't exist without the moon, but that's another class period. Today I want to discuss gravity. Back to the issue of mass. To summarize, the more mass, the more gravitational force that an object exerts. With that in mind, imagine a substance so dense that only a teaspoon of it would weigh 500 million tons on earth."

"Sounds like a cafeteria biscuit," someone said, and the class roared their appreciation, except for Sam, who was deep in thought, imagining himself sitting beside Delilah on a beach, both of them looking up at the moon. He'd whisper something into her ear, and she'd giggle. Their small fire would crackle, and then he'd lean in and kiss her gently on the cheek. She'd turn, look into his eyes, put one hand behind his neck, and pull his mouth to her lips. . . .

"All right, all right, yes, I do agree that the cafeteria biscuits are on the dense side, but I actually had something else in mind: a neutron star." Mr. Anderson added the term to his notes and continued. "Neutron stars are formed when large stars, or stars 1.4 to 3 times larger than our sun, collapse in on themselves as they exhaust their energy supplies. The extraordinary gravitational force caused by so much mass actually pushes the electrons into the nucleus. Now remember, normally that same electron would be orbiting very far away. So with all of this open space eliminated, the star, once 1.4 to 3 times the size of our sun, shrinks to a sphere only ten miles in diameter." Mr. Anderson pointed out the window. "It would be like crushing that school bus into a marble."

Normally, Sam would have found this discussion fascinating—collapsing stars, extreme forces, the prospect of earth meeting its demise in deep space. In fact, physics and astronomy were Sam's favorite subjects, and he himself hoped to one day travel to Mars. But today he was overwhelmed by Delilah. He thought about sitting next to her for the entire fourth quarter of the school year and wondered what he had done to deserve such an honor.

Although Delilah had never even looked at him and was currently dating a big shot basketball player, Sam was optimistic. *Under the right conditions*, he thought, *under the right conditions*. He just needed to be patient. After all, Rome wasn't built in a day.

Mr. Anderson remained quiet for a moment and then continued. "Now if you think that's amazing, consider this: If a star is over three times the diameter of our sun (2.5 million miles wide), the collapsing giant star has so much mass that it actually compresses itself into a point *without* dimensions, into what scientists call a singularity." After writing the word on the board, he turned back to the class. "Can anyone tell me what we have now?"

Quietly, Sam uttered a response. A few students turned and looked at him, including Delilah, who acted surprised that he was sitting so close.

Sam looked into Delilah's face, into her dark eyes, held his head up confidently, and proudly repeated his answer: “A black hole.”

“You’re right, Sam, a black hole,” commended Mr. Anderson, “the most powerful force in the universe, exerting so much gravity that it doesn’t even allow light to escape. These monsters consume entire solar systems.” After setting his chalk down, he began pacing. “Maybe you’re wondering how scientists locate black holes if they don’t give out any light. Well, this would be a more-than-legitimate question. And the answer can be found in the old proverb ‘Where there’s smoke, there’s fire.’ That is, a black hole’s effect on surrounding objects reveals its location.”

Mr. Anderson turned back to the board and wrote “Cygnus X-I: the first black hole ever discovered.” Then he turned the lights off and switched on an overhead projector.

“This, my fellow earthlings, is a black hole. In this image, you are witnessing the material of an entire solar system, like our own, being slowly devoured.”

No one said anything for the next few moments and stared at the image. Sam did the same and was surprised to find it so beautiful. The stars, planets, and cosmic debris swirling into obliteration didn't look threatening at all. In fact, the colorful streaks of light closely resembled the fluted petals of a flower.

"Notice the black region here." Mr. Anderson pointed with a meter stick. "This is called the event horizon. Once matter enters this area, it has passed the point of no return—not even light escapes from here."

"I hope we don't have one of *those* nearby," someone said.

"Not to worry. This black hole is 50 million light years from earth. That's the distance light can travel at 186, 000 miles per second for 50 million years."

With that, Mr. Anderson turned the lights back on. "We'll continue our discussion of black holes tomorrow. But right now I want you to clear your desks. Pop quiz."

The students began shuffling papers.

"It should be easy if you did last night's reading."

Sam knew all five questions, and he jotted his answers down quickly. Then he flipped his paper over and sat enjoying the idea that he was going to be sitting next to Delilah until the end of the school year. As the other students rubbed their temples, erased and then rewrote their answers, Sam imagined Delilah coming to school in summer dresses and colorful blouses. She would wear her hair up and expose her slender neck. He figured that on hot days, she would most likely wear sandals. He envisioned striking up a friendship and then maybe a romance. They would spend the entire summer together, walking on the beach, sharing a soda at the movies, driving up the coast and hiking in the mountains.

Sam was so engrossed in fantasy that he was unaware of a growing sensation on his right leg.

Yes, there it was again, a hand. Surprised, he looked down and noticed that it was certainly a hand, a hand that was connected to Delilah's arm, which was connected to her body. *Delilah's hand.*

"Hey, I don't know the answer to question three or five," Delilah whispered and smiled. She squeezed his leg again lightly and then gestured for him to turn over his quiz.

Sam looked back down at his leg, where Delilah's hand had just been resting, and then into her eyes that squinted slightly. She smiled and pursed her glossy lips. Sam looked to the front of the room where Mr. Anderson was busy grading papers. In one quick movement, he turned his quiz over and slid it in her direction. Delilah took a few glances and copied his answers.

"Thanks," she said flatly as Sam moved his paper to the left without saying anything in reply.

"Sam, Delilah—out in the hall—*now*. Bring your quizzes," came Mr. Anderson's voice. He was making his way out the door.

Sam jerked back in his seat and then looked at Delilah, who seemed suddenly angry with him. She shoved her chair in and walked past him briskly to the door.

In the hallway, Mr. Anderson stood with his back against a bank of lockers. “Okay, what’s going on? You know there’s no talking during a quiz. Who can explain the paper shuffling and conversation?”

Delilah began speaking immediately, “To be honest with you, Mr. Anderson, I had finished my quiz and was waiting for you to collect them when Sam told me that he wasn’t sure about a few of his answers. When I told him that I wouldn’t cheat, he slid his paper over and asked me to check his work.”

Mr. Anderson turned the edges of his lips down slightly and furrowed his brow. “Sam, is this correct? Did you ask Delilah for the answers?”

Sam stood silent for a moment and then looked

at Delilah. He noticed that her lips were tensing as if she were mouthing words to him. He thought that he could actually hear them, *I love you. I love you. I love you, my hero.* Then she smiled in a way that placed a dimple in her left cheek. With the back of her hand, she moved a loose strand of hair from in front of her face.

Sam felt dizzy as he faced Mr. Anderson and took a breath. "Yes, that's how it happened. I just wasn't sure about a couple of questions. It's my fault."

"Well then," began Mr. Anderson as he rubbed his chin, "I will take your quiz, Sam, and ask you to sit in the front row from now on. Cheating is serious business. You pull this in college and you'll get yourself expelled. Consider this an important life lesson."

All three of them went back into the classroom. Sam got his books and moved to the front. The students snickered as Delilah sat and checked her makeup in the mirror of her compact.

The bell rang a few minutes later, and a group of girls gathered around Delilah as she left the room.

Sam waited in his desk before he too stood and left, feeling much smaller and heavier.

LAST-MINUTE SHOPPING

Hillary didn't mind the video cameras that were mounted to the walls and ceilings. As the black-suited men had promised, they were relatively small and swiveled quietly on rotating bases. At present, they were moving back and forth over the dining room that she was so proud of. The holiday place settings and monogrammed table linens were arranged so perfectly that she hesitated before calling out to her children, "Stan Jr., Meegan, supper is ready. Be sure to wash your hands."

In the script, they were to reply courteously and

in unison, "Dearest Mother, we will be down right away."

Crossing over into the living room, Hillary lightly patted her apron that was embroidered with winter holly leaves and priced to sell at $34.95 (two for $49.99). Surprised, she discovered a friendly golden retriever curled in front of the fire and her husband Stan wearing a pair of trendy wire-rimmed glasses. He was reclined on the couch, smoking a pipe and reading a dusty novel. His feet were elevated on a leather ottoman tagged at $499. (A red line through the old price indicated that it had been reduced by almost 35%.) A pair of black monk strap loafers was neatly placed off to the side, a closeout bargain at $17.95.

"Stan, honey, supper is ready."

As if he had been suddenly broken out of deep thought, he responded, "Wonderful, dear, wonderful. I'll finish this paragraph and be in shortly."

"What are you reading?"

As Stan turned the book, Hillary realized that it was just a prop and that the pages were blank. (But it also was for sale: $12.99.)

"I'll have to read it when you're done," she said and then exited the room, the golden retriever loping at her heels.

The turkey was truly amazing, like something out of a magazine. It was already cut up. All Hillary had to do was ask Stan to serve it at the end of the table. That is, after he made a toast to the falling snow, loosened his tie ($29.95), and smiled.

On cue, both children held up their plates as Stan picked up the serving fork.

"Now, children, don't you think that your mother should have the first piece of this magnificent bird? After all, we wouldn't have such a fine meal if she hadn't worked all day to prepare it."

Stan Jr. sighed as he looked over at his younger sister. Then, as if connected together, they both turned toward Hillary and tilted their heads *slightly*, as the script had directed, and gave her exaggerated smiles of appreciation. (Hillary was suddenly glad that she'd made appointments to have their teeth whitened.)

"You're right, Father. *Mother* should have the first piece," said Stan Jr. as he reached for Hillary's plate.

Though she didn't cook any of the food, the black-suited men told Hillary to smile all the same. "What a gentleman you are, Stan Jr.," she said and handed her empty Melatina plate over the dinner rolls, making sure the price tag was visible to the cameras. "It is my pleasure to cook for such a terrific family."

At this point in their performance, Meegan was supposed to start humming a popular holiday song as they dished up the relish, marshmallow salad, green beans, garlic mashed potatoes, stuffing, and gravy. The script directed each family member to join her at certain points, so that when all of the plates were filled, everyone would be humming and looking joyful.

Their long rehearsals certainly paid off because not only was the food nicely arranged on each plate, but they perfectly harmonized the final verse of "Santa Claus Is Coming to Town," holding the last note for theatrics and then clapping for themselves.

Exactly twenty-two seconds later, a brown panel truck pulled up in front of the house, and a short man in a brown uniform walked up the steps carrying a cardboard box. He opened the door and rubbed his beard. Without speaking, the man came into the dining room, lifted the two pewter candle sticks off the table, blew out the flames, and rolled them in bubble wrap. Quickly, he boxed them, taped the lid closed, and placed a self-adherent address label on it as he made his way back to the door.

Hillary wasn't surprised that the candle sticks were the first to go. They were her favorites too, crafted by a famous French artisan with an important-sounding name. And at $99.95 a pair, they were a steal.

Breaking the uncomfortable silence left by the delivery man, Hillary questioned her son, "So, Stan Jr., what do you think Santa's going to bring you this year?"

"Mother, I would really like to have a new television for my room. Mine has such a small screen. Everyone else in my class has a 72" HD plasma flat screen with brain-interfacing technology."

"Well, I wouldn't be at all surprised if Santa were loading that television onto his sleigh right now." She paused and took a sip of water. "You *have* been a good boy this year."

"That's right, Son," Stan Sr. piped in, reaching for the jello salad. "Santa Claus rewards only good boys and girls."

"I've been good too!" interjected Meegan, her empty spoon held high like the Olympic torch.

Hillary leaned over the silver gravy boat and patted her daughter's arm. "Oh, you have been a good girl this year. You've done all of your chores, helped at the fundraising bizarre, and brought home *two* straight-A report cards. What more can parents ask for?"

Meegan smiled wide enough to reveal clumps of mashed potato still packed into her cheeks.

Neither Stan nor Hillary thought the next scene was very dramatic. It seemed forced and lacked continuity. But the men in the suits told them that everyone had to follow the script exactly the way it was written and that there were many other interested families if they could not fulfill the explicit terms of the contract. So from then on, Stan and Hillary didn't question anything. Instead, they made a point of nodding their heads from time to time and correcting the children.

Stan checked his watch and then stood up from

the table. All of the video cameras turned in his direction as he cleared his throat and began speaking. "During the holiday season, it is right to reflect on those things that we are thankful for, those things that have inspired us to be stronger, better people. We need to remember the significant parts of life that often go overlooked. Like this authentic mission style serving hutch, for example."

The stage directions instructed Stan to gently rub his left hand across the face of the hutch and then slowly down the front, revealing some of its finer features.

"Notice the hand-applied honey stain, which brings to life the wood's naturally open grain. This all-hardwood piece has beveled glass panel doors that provide a touch of elegance without muting its classic warmth. Kids, this is more than furniture. It is really an extension of our family—of who we are—we are a quality family, a *unique* family." Moving across the room, Stan continued his monologue. "And this matching wall mirror, together with our six-chair table set, makes our dining experience complete."

If Hillary hadn't been wondering why she didn't see her husband's reflection in the mirror, she would have spoiled her makeup with tears. He was doing such a good job when it counted most. In rehearsal, his hand movements looked heavy and cumbersome, but now he was moving with grace, gently framing each piece of hardware and perfectly mortised joint.

"There are many copies, but only one original," finished Stan, folding his hands together close to his chest.

A long moment passed as the children looked at their father with admiration. Hillary too was awestruck.

Stan cleared his throat and raised one eyebrow at his wife. Hillary realized that she was late with her next line and spoke hurriedly, "Stan, honey, aren't you forgetting something?" she said and nodded toward the floor.

Dropping slowly onto one knee, Stan continued. "How could I forget this plush, handmade, 100% New Zealand wool oriental rug. Just feel the imported quality as you enjoy its elaborate yet complementing design. It would complete any fine dining ensemble and comes in several popular sizes. Best of all, it's affordable, starting at only $999."

Together both children sighed deeply, "We love you so much, Father. You're the greatest. But what about financing?"

Stan parted his hands to explain. "I'm glad you asked, children, because right now all of these items are available twelve months same as cash. Not only that, but they can be delivered in time for the New Year."

Three more brown-clothed men came through the front door and took the serving hutch. They returned for the mirror and rug, which they skillfully slid from underneath the table legs. They also removed the trendy wire-rimmed glasses that Stan was now wearing low on the bridge of his nose and a porcelain evergreen tree that was serving as a centerpiece.

One of the men bumped Hillary's leg as he rolled the carpet and mumbled something. She tried not to notice and continued. "My, don't our Shaliza draperies accentuate the chair cushions and walls?"

"Yes they do," began Meegan, "and they are so soft."

"That's because they are made from the finest Pima cotton and have an extra-high thread count. These exclusive window treatments come in white, stone, cranberry, and natural. (Color-matched tie-backs included.) A great value at $75.99."

Hillary watched the men load the rug into the truck and drive away.

Stan Jr. rose from the table and stood next to the curtains. With an open hand cradling the price tag, he spoke, "Best of all, our neighbors must think we're rich."

At that moment, there was a sound of screeching tires as the brown truck braked hard and then backed its way up the street, stopping abruptly in front of the house. The three men ran up the walkway with electric screwdrivers and came into the dining room. Within minutes they had removed the drapes and curtain rods and had packed them into shipping boxes. They also removed Stan Jr.'s red v-neck sweater, which exposed his white button-down shirt that also had a price tag: $24.95.

Then they left.

"What do you say we go caroling after dinner?" asked Hillary brightly, seeing that her son had just slipped a blue pill into his mouth.

Meegan, and Stan Jr. responded enthusiastically, "Can we bring Goldie?"

Hillary had forgotten about the dog. She figured it was still in the kitchen, or perhaps it had returned to the fireplace. *What a friendly animal* was her last thought before answering. "Why not? Stan, what do you say? Will you join us?"

"Absolutely. I'll bring my accordion."

"Splendid!" said Hillary in a kind of British accent.

Suddenly music began piping in from somewhere, and both children looked up in surprise.

"That music isn't in the script," said Meegan, looking over at her father.

"CONTINUE PLEASE. CONTINUE WITH THE SCRIPT PLEASE," came a harsh voice from the ceiling.

Hillary figured the black-suited men must have felt the performance needed a little something extra. "It's nothing, honey. What songs shall we sing when we go caroling?"

"How about 'Frosty the Snowman' and 'Rudolph the Red-Nosed Reindeer'?" asked Stan Jr.

"I like those songs. Don't you, Stan?"

"Magnificent choices indeed."

The final scene called for another prolonged silence, so they dished up more food and ate quietly.

As Hillary removed the olives from her salad, she noticed that most of the video cameras were now focused on the dining room table. She wondered about that until the back door opened and slammed shut. Suddenly, a spry woman in a white lab coat shuffled into the dining room with a clipboard. She made a few notations before removing the price tag that was propped up against the salt and pepper shakers. (The new asking price was lower than Hillary expected.) The woman looked up into one of the cameras and gestured with her right hand until a loud beep came from the basement. Then she turned, hastily adjusted the red bow in Meegan's hair, and disappeared into the kitchen.

She left a few minutes later, carrying the golden

retriever under one arm.

"I really like hot chocolate. Can we bring some when we go caroling?" asked Meegan in response to the grandfather clock that began to chime in the hallway.

"We certainly can," responded Stan Sr. "You know, hot chocolate reminds me of my own childhood, growing up in West Virginia. Yes, we used to take long horse-drawn carriage rides up into the mountains and sip hot chocolate with marshmallows as the snow fell all around us. Why, it was much like the scene depicted in that original print hanging above our vintage wine rack. The piece, entitled *Going Home*, is a fine example of Seymour Mershall's earlier mountain work and is now on sale for just $119.95, plus tax and shipping."

"I wish *we* could go for a horse-drawn carriage ride," pouted Meegan lightly.

"That would be nice, dear," began Hillary as she stood and walked over to the painting, "but we have the next best thing, this signed and numbered, limited edition collector's print, which is available in several mattes and frames and, for a very limited time, comes with this handsome brass plaque at no additional charge."

As her family began clapping, the brown truck appeared out in front of the house. This time the somber-faced men hoisted the entire dining room table—turkey and all—onto their shoulders. They carried it right out the front door and came back for the chairs, Hillary's short-heeled dress shoes, Meegan's red bow, the painting, and Stan Sr.'s holiday tie. They also took a very realistic-looking silk plant that had been positioned in the corner and two wrought-iron wall sconces, the absence of which brought out shadows and made the room a little darker.

When the truck drove away, Hillary looked down at her son, who sat on the bare hardwood floor with a half-eaten turkey leg in his hand. "What do you say we have some dessert?"

In accord, her family mustered muted cheers that now echoed in the near-empty room. Hillary went into the kitchen and brought out a silver platter layered with holiday favorites. She also brought decaf for Stan and milk for the kids.

"Well, I suppose this is as good a time as any," said Stan Sr.

"A good time for what?" asked Hillary, faking surprise.

Stan took a small box out of his pocket. "For this. Happy holidays, dear."

The children beamed, and Hillary gasped, "Oh, Stan, you shouldn't have." She took the box into her hands and loosened the silver ribbon that was tied up into a bow. Carefully, she opened the felt-covered lid and put her open hand up to her pursed mouth. "This is too much, a diamond tennis bracelet! It's too much! Kids, look at how beautiful it is. This three-carat total diamond weight bracelet is set in lustrous 14K white gold and shined to perfection." After holding the price tag up to the cameras, she continued. "It means that your father truly loves me. See how it sparkles." Hillary carefully lifted the bracelet and asked her son to clasp it. She turned it on her wrist a few times and smiled as she bit into a coconut fudge bar.

When the men came back, they removed the remaining items: an evergreen wreath, the teak wine rack, nostalgic black and white photos of strangers, the silver platter of cookies, and the brass chandelier, which left them without light and at the end of the script.

They sat in the dark without saying anything, waiting for something to happen. Hillary assumed the black-suited men would return now and explain what to do next. But instead, another truck stopped in front of the house.

The front door opened, and Hillary heard footsteps. A rough hand unclasped the diamond bracelet from her wrist. And then she heard some rustling and lifting before the front door slammed shut.

After the truck drove away, a long moment passed before Hillary felt comfortable enough to speak. "Stan? Stan? Meegan? Stan Jr.? Hello?"

She reached across the floor, waving her hands wildly. But they were gone. Yelling at the ceiling, Hillary demanded to know what was going on, using words like "freedom," "liberty," and "rights." But when nothing happened, she started screaming and crying until she heard the familiar sound of a truck, coming to an abrupt stop in front of her house.

BLAMEMASTER 2000

The machine chirped and clicked again. Paul Norder saw a message flashing on the screen, but he couldn't read what it said. Mrs. Leafy, the secretary, a frail older woman with streaks of blue in her hair, crossed the room and turned a dial. Then she took her seat and continued sorting mail and taking phone calls.

Today, Paul was the only one hooked up to the Blamemaster 2000. Normally, there were at least a few other junior high students with their heads under the clear plastic neurodomes (a recent upgrade from the model 1000 domes that were solid black).

He figured their absence was due to a number of factors: It was Monday morning after a long weekend, holiday break was fast approaching, and he was pretty sure that Mrs. Clay, the principal, had scheduled a science assembly that afternoon. But Paul hadn't done anything interesting over the weekend, and his family didn't celebrate Christmas. Furthermore, he wasn't the slightest bit interested in watching a grown man named "Science Chuck" run around the gymnasium like an over-sugared child. No, on this particular Monday morning, Paul had his mind set on flooding the second floor bathroom, and that is exactly what he'd accomplished—and would have gotten away with if Mr. Malone hadn't walked in and actually witnessed him going from stall to stall, flushing the toilets stopped up with paper.

Mrs. Clay came out of her office and checked

the computer printout that had coiled itself like a register receipt. "Humph," she said under her breath and made a few sharp notations on a clipboard. Without making eye contact with him, she grabbed Paul's hand roughly and adjusted the probe attached to his left index finger. She tapped the plastic dome a few times and then spoke harshly to Mrs. Leafy. "Did you ever make that call to BM Enterprises?"

Her secretary nodded without looking up. Paul thought about asking Mrs. Clay what the computer said, but he could tell that she was angry this morning. Her cheeks were twitching, and she was walking at a slight angle.

Paul had overheard his parents talking about how Mrs. Clay was opposed to the new responsibility machines. She had also spoken out against the metal detectors and surveillance cameras. But in order to keep her job, she had to comply with the new state laws that required all Illinois public schools to install metal detectors and to have staffed video surveillance (in addition, of course, to the newest Blamemaster technology, which was rumored by some to have suspicious business connections to a certain congressman).

The Blamemaster was really an ingenious invention, and more and more parents and schools were beginning to praise it. The machine's inventor, Dr. Gray, built his first working model while on a work visa from France. As a psychiatrist, he had studied the areas of the human brain responsible for making bad choices. Naturally, he worked with adolescents to assemble his extensive research and then applied for an educational grant through one of America's largest teachers' unions. He was given five years and six and a half million dollars to construct a prototype.

Since then Dr. Gray had become a regular commentator for the network news stations and had been featured on several talk shows. His invention and research had been written up in many notable science, educational, and popular magazines—he even made the cover of *Our Time,* blindfolded with his hands outspread like the scales of justice. Dr. Gray really became a kind of minor celebrity, serving as the keynote speaker at functions across the country. (It seemed he had only a few critics, most of whom lived in the Midwest and were labeled by the media as old-fashioned and professionally out of date.)

At the beginning of the year, every student at Paul's school was sent home with a tri-fold pamphlet and letter from the principal that explained how the responsibility machines worked. The documents stressed that the Blamemaster was non-invasive, pain free, and totally safe. It was endorsed by OSHA, the APA, and the NEA. Even the President of the United States had included a comment about its value in her State of the Union Address, noting that it represented the "next major evolutionary leap in education."

Basically, the Blamemaster could determine where a bad choice came from. Using special sensors and three-dimensional triangulation, the machine could pinpoint poor behavior and, on that basis, determine if a student should be held responsible for his or her actions. If, for example, a student were to throw a sharpened pencil in class or leave a trail of shredded paper down the hallway or splash a group of students by jumping into a mud puddle, the Blamemaster would go to work, locating the origin of this poor behavior. First, it would scan the part of the brain that Dr. Gray's research team found to represent free choice, or the "freech zone," a relatively small area of brain tissue located just behind the left eye. If the computer were unable to detect any activity, the student would be considered a helpless victim of Random and Inexplicable Neuro Firing Syndrome, or RINFS. Such students would not be blamed for their actions but instead required to undergo a full body scan designed to pinpoint the damaged neuron(s) responsible for the poor behavior. A special pill would then be used to temporarily repair the defective neurological site—however, due to RINFS's incurability, those diagnosed with the ailment would need to take this medication for the rest of their lives.

The first time Paul was scanned by a Blamemaster, he had been systematically rearranging the library shelves. One by one, he managed to slowly disperse nonfiction card catalog numbers 130.11–300.21. Over several months, he randomly moved these books about the library, mixing them first with the reference materials and then with the popular fiction and magazines. When he got bored with that, he began dropping them behind a shelf that started to lean and eventually fell over—that's when he got caught. One of the surveillance cameras recorded him placing the last fateful book behind that wooden shelf just as it tottered over and broke to pieces on the library floor.

Mrs. Clay immediately connected Paul to a shiny new Blamemaster and ran a full scan. Amazingly, his freech zone was completely clear. The machine didn't find any evidence to indict him. Instead, the onboard computer began to hum softly as it probed through the long line of neurotransmitters, branching out in his body. After twenty minutes, it located the source of Paul's poor behavior, near his right kneecap.

Later that same afternoon, the school psychologist explained to Mr. and Mrs. Norder how neurons often get stress fractures (especially as a child passes through adolescence) and that the prescription medicine Enablar worked to repair this damage. His parents were quick to agree and after signing a six-page liability waiver, received a bottle of blue pills. (The next day, Paul no longer had an urge to rearrange the library shelves.)

Since then hundreds of students had been hooked up to one of the many Blamemaster neurodomes lining an entire wall in the main office. They had been convicted of everything from pulling fire alarms to desk graffiti. Surprisingly, none of the students were responsible for their actions. Their freech zones were clear of all malice of forethought (adding to the mounting evidence that all people are generally good, another of Dr. Gray's popular theories). Instead, the Blamemaster found scores of damaged neurons that caused students to make poor choices, damage that the Gray Research Institute attributed to the use of absolute words such as "truth," fresh air, and green vegetables.

As more and more students took the blue pills, the principal's office became less crowded. Once loud and rowdy kids became as placid and cordial as purebred show dogs—except Paul, that is. He was a loyal and repeat customer. No matter how many pills he took or how high the dose, he continued to make poor choices. True, he never had the urge to commit the *same* crime, but he was still driven to break the rules and cause general mayhem. Paul was simply forced to be more creative, like melting crayons on the radiators, popping up floor tiles, and planting hair in the cafeteria food (finding particular joy in smuggling preserved insects out of biology, which he later glued onto locker doors). Yet, the Blamemaster never found him guilty, a spotless freech zone every time.

The computer finished scanning Paul again, and Mrs. Clay came out of her office. She tore the computer printout from the machine and examined it closely. Then she crumpled it up and tossed it over her shoulder. Mrs. Leafy looked up momentarily and then started to lick postage stamps for a large stack of report cards. Paul stared down at his shoes.

"This is ridiculous," Mrs. Clay said as she hastily reset the machine and adjusted the dials. "Over three hundred kids and not one of them is responsible. Hair pulling, food throwing, name calling and cursing, stealing, cheating, backtalking, and bathroom flooding!" With that, Mrs. Clay spun around and looked into Paul's eyes that were now peering out from underneath a neurodome. She crossed the room and got right into his face. Paul could smell her foul breath when she spoke. "I know that you meant to plug those toilets. Do you know how long it will take to clean up that mess? Maybe you would like to go downstairs and see how that water destroyed the ceiling tiles in the kindergarten classrooms. Or maybe you just don't even care you little. . . ." She paused, holding a clenched fist in the air. "I'm certain that this machine must be broken. I can see it in your eyes. You knew what you were doing, and I'm not letting you off with a bottle of blue pills. You're serving *time* for this. Saturday detention. No recess for a month. If it were up to me, I'd keep you in isolation for the rest of the year." Then she squinted her eyes and growled, "I only wish they still let us paddle."

Mrs. Clay's face was flushed and shaking now. Paul could see large veins bulging up out of her forehead and red lines extending into the center of her eyes. He sat perfectly still and then shrugged his shoulders.

"I don't care if I have to test your freech zone all day. I'll prove that you're the one to blame for those toilets! I let the library book incident go, the poisoned goldfish, and the cafeteria gravy—There's no way I'll let you get away with those toilets! Understand? Answer me! *Do-you-un-der-stand?*"

Paul managed a quiet "yes" and then looked back down at the floor.

"Mrs. Leafy, see to it that Mr. Norder here stays on the Blamemaster all day if he has to. Contact me if it detects any activity in his freech."

The morning passed slowly. Several students came through the office and wondered why Paul was still attached to the Blamemaster. When they asked, the secretary would snap her fingers coldly and point to the door.

Lunch came and went, and Mrs. Leafy continued to reset the machine that maintained his innocence.

When the final bell rang, Paul didn't move. He sat there, waiting for Mrs. Clay to dismiss him. At 3:30 Mrs. Leafy quietly put on her thin sweater, reset the machine a final time, and then left, gently closing the door behind her.

Paul was alone now and didn't hear anything in the hallway. The buses left. Parents loaded their children into minivans, and the parking lot emptied. The only sound came from the Blamemaster, drumming out figures on the screen and flashing prognosis charts.

Fifteen minutes later, Paul heard footsteps. He saw the knob turn and in walked Mrs. Clay, carrying what looked like a broom handle. She crossed the office and examined the long tape of Blamemaster reports wound into a large pile on the floor. She shook her head and bit the inside of her cheek as she looked down the paper. After examining the final report, she bellowed like a mad cow.

Paul jerked back in his seat.

"Well, Mr. Paul Norder, it appears as if the Blamemaster finds you innocent. I suppose I can't hold you accountable for the flooded bathroom. Says that you have a bruised transmitter at the tip of your nose and that you need a prescription of Enablar (150 mg)." She tapped the broom handle into the palm of her free hand and paced back and forth in front of him. "But you know what I think?

Huh? You know what I really, truly think? I think that this machine is broken. Yep, I think that your freech zone is filled with every clever plot that has made my life difficult. I think all of your disrespectful stunts are packed in that head of yours like, like, like piñata candy, and if this machine can't beat them out of you, maybe I should."

Paul looked up through the neurodome at Mrs. Clay, approaching like a cat. He pulled his knees up to his chest and covered his eyes—then he heard shattering glass.

When he finally worked up the courage to look through his parted fingers, Paul witnessed Principal Clay swinging at the Blamemaster mainframe with the wooden pole. She jabbed at the computer monitor like a lion tamer and knocked the switches and dials onto the floor, chuckling in a deep, hearty tone. She shattered the plastic domes and tore loose the seat cushions with her hands and teeth. Finally, she stood before Paul and raised the clear dome over his head. She peeled his hands from his face and spoke in a congested, nasal tone, "That's what I think of the Blamemaster, Mr. Norder. Bruised transmitter—nonsense, utter nonsense!" And with that, she reached out in a businesslike way and pinched the very tip of Paul's nose.

He felt nothing at first and then an intense flash of heat.

The welt that formed at the end of Paul's nose immediately drew the attention of his parents, who phoned the police.

Within the hour, Mrs. Clay was taken into custody and eventually stood before a circuit court judge, who shook his head as if to say, *How could you?* But Mrs. Clay's attorney argued that she didn't know what she was doing. She wasn't in control of her actions, and it wasn't her fault. The honorable Alfonz P. Bableton thought about that for a moment and then signaled to the bailiff.

The following day in court, a Blamemaster was set up in front of the bench. An actual representative from BM Enterprises was present to set the necessary switches and dials. He attached the finger probe and then lowered the neurodome over Mrs. Clay's head. The courtroom was silent as the computer scanned her freech zone. After a few minutes, it printed a diagnostic chart, which the technician looked over and then handed to the judge.

"Well, Mrs. Clay, the Blamemaster hasn't found you guilty of any wrongdoing, so I suppose I cannot either. You're free to go, pending your treatment with Enablar."

Mrs. Clay wept as she thanked the judge and BM technician, who handed her a large bottle of blue pills.

Paul and his family also felt much better knowing the principal hadn't actually meant any harm and that her pinching him was really due to an illness, a deviated synaptic crossover in one of her toes.

Three weeks later, Mrs. Clay was back at school and considerably thinner. She laughed a lot now and even slapped her own knee from time to time. Perhaps the biggest change, however, was in the way she treated the students. Instead of looking at them bitterly and chiding them with harsh words, she smiled, crooning friendly remarks: "Oh, you have a great day now." "What a nice outfit you have on." "What a glorious afternoon and what glorious students." Even to the kids who were caught breaking the rules, she had only kind words and friendly pats on the back. No matter the crime, Mrs. Clay reacted the same way. She would run the necessary Blamemaster scan (The school's machines had been replaced and upgraded free of charge by BM Enterprises.) and then invite them to recline on her futon with a can of soda or an ice cream cone while they took their first dose of Enablar, which she now dispensed from a vending machine in her office.

Over time, there were fewer and fewer things to do wrong. Enablar had systematically removed any desire to repeat poor behavior. Even the notorious Paul Norder had trouble finding rules to break. He became so desperate that he was reduced to pulling up carpet snags and throwing what little wax he managed to scrape out of his ears. Yet each time Mrs. Clay ran the Blamemaster scan, she smiled and told him how much she cared about him and wanted his behavior to improve. Then she'd hand him more pills.

And eventually Paul's behavior *did* change. It took another year and a half, but his attitude finally improved dramatically. Paul had literally run out of things to do wrong. He was cured. He started to think friendly thoughts and even picked a bouquet of dandelions for Mrs. Clay on the last day of school.

Post Script

Soon everyone at Paul's junior high school was taking Enablar: the students, the teachers, even the cooks who now volunteered their time on Saturday to make fresh apple cobblers. The newspapers were calling it a miracle, and Dr. Gray proclaimed that it was only the beginning. "Every school should model itself after this fine institution. We owe it to the future of our country to make Blamemasters and Enablar a part of *every* school."

Ten years later, more than half of the world's population took Enablar on a daily basis. Global peace seemed a real possibility. What was once only a trite comment made at beauty pageants appeared actually possible for the first time. Countries voluntarily dismantled their militaries and destroyed their bombs in public gatherings organized by the Do-Good International Committee. Standing armies baked bread. And tanks were hollowed out and used as flower beds.

Two large factories kept the entire world supplied with Enablar. Freighters filled with blue pills crossed the Atlantic and Pacific oceans. Train cars bearing the pill's trademark crisscrossed the seven continents.

Then it was suggested that Enablar become a mandatory ingredient in milk and injected into livestock. Crop seeds were soaked in Enabler baths before planting season. Now, the need to remember a pill was eliminated because Enablar was in everything: candy, produce, cheese, potato chips, meat, soda, water—it was even atomized and released into the air over cities.

Soon history books began referring to Enablar as the wonder drug of the millennium and hailed Dr. Gray, a hero.

Even the ozone layer was beginning to close.

HARD SELL

They appeared textbook: four-bedroom colonial with a fenced yard, 2½ baths, attached garage, and a minivan in the driveway. A polished brass doorknocker read "*The Jones's*." He was probably a mid-level manager and she a stay-at-home mom. With this in mind, Norm began with the responsible-young-man-raising-money-for-college pitch. But when he noticed that it was having no effect, he conspicuously fanned out the neighbors' checks, the everyone-else-is-doing-it routine. Nothing. They didn't say anything, just stood there in the doorway with transparent smiles, nodding.

Was he losing his touch? Were his days of vacationing on sales bonuses over? Did he have something on his face? Between his teeth?

"Tell you what I'm gonna do," Norm continued with renewed vigor. "I like you folks, so I'm going to include—at no additional charge—this handy bottle brush and our patented Mug Bug as well."

The Joneses showed no interest, only looked out at the street, where a passing car swerved suddenly to avoid hitting a squirrel. Then Mr. Jones checked his watch, thanked Norm for his time, and began to shut the door.

Under pressure, Norm reached deep inside himself and quickly gathered up all of his sales training, every seminar and article, every episode of his favorite cable program *Always Closing*. He concentrated and felt a surge of superhuman strength before he poured out a sales litany that blanketed every known customer profile. From save-money-by-using-concentrated-soap to imagine-how-nice-your-kitchen-sink-will-smell and everything in between. He wrote on his arm with a permanent marker and proudly lathered up Citrus Burst Miracle Soap to wipe it clean. Walla, no more writing! But the Joneses weren't impressed, so Norm took the same marker to his white oxford and lifted the stain with a triumphant grin.

Again, stone cold.

"This is a permanent marker, Mrs. Jones," he reminded her. But there wasn't a twitch, not a single artificial smile—*nothing* on either of their faces. They weren't going to budge, so Norm brought out the heavy guns and began to fake pain in his abdomen. "Oh, it's nothing. I'll be fine. No need to worry. One of these days, I'll be able to afford the operation," he moaned and then coughed dramatically. "It's not so bad, really. Doctor says I still have some time."

Mrs. Jones disappeared down the hall and returned with a can of ginger ale, which Norm accepted with a smile. He took this as a sign that they were finally beginning to soften. But when he took his first sip, Mr. Jones curtly thanked him again and shut the door.

No, no, no, Norm thought to himself as he looked into the sky. He rubbed his forehead and noticed a black kite. He turned back to the door. "Always closing, always closing, *always* closing," he chanted softly. Norm inhaled through his nostrils and rapped the brass knocker three times. He heard some footsteps, and the door opened. This time a little girl looked up at him. She had a pony tail off the right side of her head and held a blue crayon.

"Hi there," Norm said. "What's your name?"

She stared back at him and squinted. "Madelyn, and I'm four years old," she said, indicating the number of years with her fingers.

"Well, Madelyn, who's four years old, are your parents home?"

The girl nodded, turned, and ran into the house screaming, “Mom, Dad, it’s for you!”

A few moments later, Mr. Jones returned to the door, followed by his wife who held a wooden spoon in her hand.

“Did I mention how well Citrus Burst Miracle Soap works on crayon stains? I see that you have a little one. Well, as parents, you no doubt understand how kids like to color on walls and couch cushions. But with the power of citrus, folks, you have nothing to worry about—you can cut right through the most ground-in crayon marks.”

Mr. and Mrs. Jones looked at him blankly. They stared like undertakers and took the same poses they had earlier, except now the little girl was standing between their legs and trying to lick the wooden spoon that Norm assumed to be covered with cookie dough.

“Oh, yes, it will take crayon off painted surfaces, wallpaper, hardwood floors, metal, glass, plastic, ceramic, and virtually every kind of carpet—guaranteed! If you're not *completely* satisfied, Citrus Burst Miracle Soap Incorporated will refund 100% of your money and provide you with reduced-price tickets to the zoo. So what'll it be, the twelve, twenty-four, or thirty-six ounce container?"

Mr. Jones raised a single eyebrow and then looked at his wife.

"Oh, I know you're the kind of man who buys in bulk. Smart. Well, I just happen to have an entire gallon of Citrus Burst Miracle Soap in my car over there. It's my last one, but I'm going to sell it to you fine folks." With that, Norm hastily wrote up a sales ticket for the full amount and presented the triplicate carbon form to Mr. Jones, who looked at it oddly.

"Now, did you want to pay by cash, check, or credit card? Believe it or not, I can accept all major credit cards, for your convenience. All you need to do is fill in the lower portion of the form with your account information. I'll take care of the rest."

After blinking a few times, Mr. Jones thanked Norm in the same brisk way he had earlier and shut the door. The little girl peeked through one of the sidelight windows and then disappeared.

Norm stood there for a few moments in disbelief—he hadn't lost a sale in three years. He'd broken every sales record that Citrus Burst had ever recorded. He trained the new employees and had written many of the training manuals. He taught salesmen how to "read" a family. He coined the word "profily," a term he used when describing the marketing profile of a family. He had even begun to collect his notes for a book-length manuscript, which he planned to title *Selling Oceanfront Property in Alabama: The Definitive Guide to High-Pressure Sales*.

Now he was standing in front of a door that had been closed in his face. Part of him wanted to knock a third time, but he didn't. Maybe this was just some kind of anomaly like the Bermuda Triangle. Every salesman, no matter how skilled, was bound to come up against such a family now and again. Nothing was wrong with him. He had been sales leader since December, and the local paper was doing an editorial about his upcoming "Super Sales Seminar." He was Norm B. Hallow, Sales Professional. No, nothing was wrong with him.

And this is what he told himself on his way to the car, where he took his demonstration bottle of Citrus Burst Miracle Soap and tossed it on the passenger seat. He sat behind the wheel and started the engine. The radio came on playing a country western song that began tightening the muscles in his neck:

I'm a loser, but you love me,
you love me, you love me.
I'm a loser, but you love me,
you love me all the same.

Norm shut the motor off and looked into the rearview mirror. He fixed his hair and mumbled a few encouraging words to himself. After clearing his throat, he gathered his clipboard and soap and shuffled back up the brick walkway. At the door, he confidently knocked with his own knuckles, four short raps, just above the doorknob. He heard footsteps.

As he waited, Norm repeated the words of his mentor, Melinda "Sales Queen" Fernandez, who had retired early from Citrus and now owned a resort village in the Bahamas: "Everyone needs something, everyone needs something, *everyone* needs something." But Norm understood that he was entering uncharted water. He had already tapped the extent of his sales training, and the Joneses hadn't taken the bait. He didn't even sense a hairline crack in their demeanor but faced the same plastic smiles every time he tried to finalize the deal.

Norm didn't know what he was going to do but trusted that he would know soon. The moment that door opened, he would understand how to sell the Joneses. One thing was certain—he was going to leave with one less bottle of Citrus Burst Miracle Soap!

Mrs. Jones answered the door this time, and without even saying a word to her, Norm took three solid gulps of the orange soap. It ran down his cheeks and onto his shirt. When he spoke, bubbles formed in the corners of his mouth.

"Mrs. Jones, we're really talking about safety here. This cleaner is powerful on dirt but safe enough to drink," Norm stated confidently, feeling a nauseous ache welling up into his throat. "I can drink this all day, and it won't hurt me." He took another couple of mouthfuls and continued. "With children around, you need to be worried about dangerous chemicals under your sink. But Citrus Burst Miracle Soap is harmless, harmless as tap water."

Then he hiccuped and burped lightly out the side of his mouth.

Something truly had come over Norm. He was working an angle that had never been explored before, and it was having an effect. He was certain that Mrs. Jones widened her eyes just a little when he wiped his mouth clean with the back of his hand. She was buying this safety pitch. So he continued.

"You can even pour this stuff on open cuts, and you won't feel a thing." With that, Norm cocked his arm back and drove a roundhouse punch into his closed mouth, which began to bleed down his chin.

"See, watch this," Norm murmured past his numb lip and the searing pain in his cheek while he splashed handfuls of the orange soap on his face like aftershave. "I can put Citrus Burst Miracle Soap all over these cuts and not feel a thing. Bet you don't have any cleaners like *that* under your kitchen sink. Nope, Citrus Burst Miracle Soap is truly one of a kind."

Between the gurgling in his stomach and the swelling of his mouth (and now the stinging of his open wounds covered with citrus oil), Norm felt like a prize fighter halfway through the seventh round, but he continued as he had taught so many other young and determined salesmen to do. He focused on the sale. He spoke quickly and resolutely without giving Mrs. Jones an opportunity to refuse. *He* was in control.

When Mr. Jones suddenly appeared in the doorway, Norm thought of another brilliant idea and splashed some of the soap into his eyes. That made him double over and almost cry out, but he didn't. Instead, he straightened himself and patted his eyes with a tissue.

"Mr. Jones, I was just telling your wife here that Citrus Burst Miracle Soap is safe and non-toxic. Don't have to worry about little Madelyn getting into any dangerous cleaners. Not with Citrus Burst Miracle Soap."

At this point something led Norm to transition into bacteria and the dangers of food poisoning. He began to explain how food particles become a breeding ground for bacteria, some deadly.

"Sir, you look like the type of man who enjoys a steak from time to time. Hey, who doesn't like barbecue? Well did you know that food particles can actually grow bacteria on dirty cooking surfaces? Oh yeah, nastiest little critters you've ever seen, but this Citrus Burst Miracle Soap will clean'em right up. You don't want anyone in your family getting sick from a dirty grill, Mr. Jones. And you *don't* want to mess with bacteria. You may not be able to see them, but they can still harm you. Have you ever seen magnified bacteria? Ugly, ugly, ugly. Look like this." Quickly, Norm crouched down and held his arms lurching out in front of himself, opening and closing his hands like a lobster. "Bacteria, you see, actually pinch the lining of your stomach, and that's what makes you sick." Then he stopped abruptly. "But I don't want to give you a science lesson. I just want to make sure that your family's protected."

This time, Mrs. Jones slammed the door without saying anything. It shut harder than before, and the brass knocker came off the base, making a single rap like a judge's gavel.

Norm was alone again, but now he had a belly full of Citrus Burst, a bruise forming on his right cheek, a couple of loose teeth, and a growing twitch in his neck—but he kept talking. He wasn't going to give up. Life was a challenge, but when the going got tough, the tough got going. *Carpe Diem!*

They just need to see Citrus Burst Miracle Soap in action, that's all, Norm thought and began making his way to the backyard. He scaled the slat board fence and dropped down with both feet into a flowerbed. Like a trained soldier, he scoped the backyard and spotted his target, the grill, positioned on an angle in the corner of the deck. Breathing out of his pursed lips, Norm squinted his eyes that had begun to tear uncontrollably and marched forward, over a sandbox, islands of ground cover, and a small goldfish pond.

On the deck, Norm looked up and saw the Joneses looking at him through an upstairs window. Their heads were crowded together like gathered balloons, and that made him think of the circus. That's all selling was truly about, smoke and mirrors, a high-wire act with a net, a magic show. The trick was always finding the *right* trick, and he knew that he had it this time. The Joneses were a hands-on type of family. No talk. They wanted to *see* Citrus Burst Miracle Soap in action.

He yelled up to them after tilting the lid back, "You hear that! I'm going to give you some serious cleaning action! You'll see! When I'm done with this grill, you'll beg me for Citrus Burst Miracle Soap!" Then Norm let out a maniacal laugh and set to work, scrubbing the grime off the Jones's grill.

First he chiseled off the hardened chunks of meat and baked-on fat drippings. Then he soaked the entire grill, inside and out, with Citrus Burst. As part of his routine in these types of demonstrations, he consulted his watch as he dramatically counted down one minute, emphasizing the last ten seconds as if he were approaching the New Year.

"That's all it takes, folks, one minute, a single minute for Citrus Burst Miracle Soap to break up all that grime, which is then simply . . . wiped away."

Norm reached into his back pocket and pulled out the small square towel that he kept for just such occasions. He began wiping the top and worked down to the base and the two small plastic wheels. All the while, he hummed the most recent Citrus Burst jingle that had been airing on local radio stations.

When he finished, Norm turned the grill to give

the Joneses a better view. He opened the lid and pointed to where some of the more tenacious grime had been lodged. Then he cradled the bottle of orange soap in the cup of his right hand, resting it back into his left. He presented it the way they do on television in order to make the soap seem exclusive and valuable.

The Joneses had moved to a different window now, and Mrs. Jones held a phone to her ear. Norm could see that the little girl was crying and that Mr. Jones was speaking to his wife in a hurried way. Maybe they were inviting some friends over to witness the miracle that Norm had managed to work on the grill. Yes, that was it, they just couldn't wait to tell people about this revolutionary cleaner.

"Hey, you think that's impressive, I'll show you impressive. Did I mention that Citrus Burst Miracle soap works on glass? Does it ever. Dries streak-free too."

As he began scaling the downspout, Norm continued. "See that window that you're looking out of? I bet you also see the unsightly film of dirt that can accumulate after a long winter. Well, Citrus Burst Miracle Soap will cut right through that dirt and leave your windows with a sparkle." Just as he said those words, Norm lost his footing and tore loose a support bracket from the vinyl siding. But he continued on and used his bottle of soap as a climbing hold, incrementally wedging it against the house.

Norm looked up and decided that he would need his belt to swing in front of the window ledge where the Joneses were about to see his culminating sales maneuver. Only inches from their faces, they would understand what Citrus Burst Miracle Soap was capable of, and then he would take their money and zip it into his green nylon deposit bag, go home victorious, and enjoy a bologna sandwich in front of the TV. He only had a few more feet to go.

Suddenly, Norm heard a voice below him,

"There he is up on the gutter. He's almost to the top. Hey, you, don't go any farther! We have the entire house surrounded. You have nowhere to run."

Norm looked down and saw a group of police officers spreading out over the yard. The one who spoke to him was cupping his hands in front of his mouth like a megaphone. "Now, I want you to come down from there, sir, slowly, no sudden movements. Understand? Just back down the gutter the way you went up. No one's going to hurt you. Come down and talk to us. We want to help you."

They wanted to help him? Norm looked confused but figured that Mr. Jones was a police officer or, more likely, the police chief, and that he had invited the entire station over to take advantage of this spectacular deal. No, he was going to help *them*. (Perhaps Mr. Jones thought that he would get in on some of the commission if he roped in a few more customers. That thought made Norm chuckle to himself.)

"Don't worry boys, don't worry, there's plenty of Citrus Burst Miracle Soap for everyone. I have an entire car full. There's no need to get greedy." With those words, Norm began to lower himself, whispering random scripted sales pitches: "Value, value—one capful does the trick. One bottle lasts an entire year. Blast dirt with the power of citrus. Smells clean and fruity too."

When he got to the bottom, a few of the officers tackled Norm to the ground and cuffed his arms behind his back. They hauled him to his feet, read him his rights, and led him toward a fence gate, held open by a young, female officer.

Norm noticed her earrings right away. "Don't even get me started on jewelry. Citrus Burst Miracle Soap will shine up the dullest silver and truly bring to life all of your precious gems and family heirlooms. But how rude of me. I haven't even introduced myself. Norm B. Hallow is my name, and have I got a deal for you today—more of an opportunity really. See, I like you, so I'll tell you what I'm gonna do. I notice that many of you have guns. And as I look down the barrels, I see all kinds of tarnish and grime, maybe even some bacteria. . . .

KITE DAY

I'm sure Billy Bloom had no idea that he was standing in a den of lions—hungry lions. Slouched there at the front of our sixth grade class with bits of hay in his matted hair and reeking of manure, he introduced himself and told us about his old school down south. Casually, he hitched his thumbs in his pockets, rocked back and forth on his heels, and bragged about a hog competition that he won at some county fair. Then he smiled, a goofy kind of smile that revealed a jagged chip in his front right tooth.

On and on he went, telling us how cows give birth and when to harvest tobacco. He listed specifications for several farm implements, sang a twangy folk song, and then pulled a pocket knife from his sock to describe how farmers castrate piglets. I'll never forget how quickly Ms. Gamora snatched that knife away before she patted Billy's arm and nudged him toward a desk in the back row.

No, Billy never stood a chance in sixth grade.

One of my high school history teachers would later use the word "hierarchy" to describe society in the Dark Ages. As he drew a large pyramid on the blackboard, he explained that this strange-sounding word was not some kind of kung-fu expletive, as one boy had guessed with a smirk, but was instead a power structure or a pecking order. In this case, the pecking order of an entire culture. To further illustrate this point, he divided the pyramid into horizontal cross sections, like rungs on a ladder, and explained that people who lived during medieval times believed that everything and everyone in the universe existed within such a fixed structure. Least significant and most abundant were minerals, so they were at the bottom. Then came plants, then animals, then peasants, landowners, nobility, royalty, the king, angels, and lastly God who ruled supreme at the very top.

Looking back, I understand now that we sixth-grade boys at Sunnyside Elementary had a similar hierarchy that we called popularity, and although we kept no formal list, every boy knew his place—and every other boy's place—on the pyramid. Brandon McAllister, for example, remained somewhere at the top because his older sister was the most beautiful girl in town. Even though he wore glasses, sniffled a lot, and occasionally picked flowers on the playground, Brandon possessed what could be described as a hereditary title, a royal blood line. His sister was Lily McAllister, the red-haired knockout whose long spiraling ringlets, soft features, and coy smile left an indelible impression in the mind. Everyone—male and female, old and young alike—was equally drawn in by her unique beauty. And it was because of this singular fact that Brandon was invited to every birthday party, chosen to play recess football, and often patted on the shoulder by teachers. Dale Glover, on the other hand, began near the top of the pyramid because he was so tall. But when his growth slowed in fourth grade, and he came to school with a boil on the tip of his nose, he quietly slipped several notches and ultimately graduated from Sunnyside a common, everyday peasant. Bret Ferrell really should have been at the bottom because he lived in the trailer park with his grandmother, but he entertained us. He could dislocate many of his joints and routinely wowed us by slapping live bees and making impressive noises in his pants (always during quiet time or a spelling test or when the uptight nature lady came with her caged lizards). And then there was Shazzy Baldwin. He moved to the Midwest from California, where he had spent most of his time surfing. Shazzy hardly spoke, but he had muscles, real muscles, blond hair, and long eyelashes, so he escaped the isolated life of most new kids. I still remember how the girls looked in awe every time he'd perform some kind of acrobatic maneuver on the jungle gym or turn up the corner of his mouth and give them a smile. They'd giggle trying to decide which Hollywood actor he resembled.

And so it was that every other boy's position was determined by such uncontrollable and often mysterious circumstances that were ultimately guided by three simple, yet unspoken, rules: (1) Learn your place. (2) *Stay* in your place. And (3) If you're lucky enough to move up a rung or two—hold on as tight as you can. And there *were* those fortunate enough to actually climb up the pyramid.

Like when Greg Marshal kissed Patricia Webber in the back of the bus. After giving us the details in the bathroom, he was suddenly elevated, lifted up from among the pool of commoners and granted a kind of permanent knighthood. (It also didn't hurt that he proved, once and for all, that he could urinate farther and higher than anyone else.).

Yet, most rises in popularity were only temporary and may have resulted from a boy wearing new clothes, catching a particularly long pass on the playground, or bringing an expensive gadget to school. The hard and honest truth was that most of us stayed wherever we found ourselves, happy there was at least one unfortunate kid a rung below.

When we weren't calling him "Fatty," "Porker," "Dough Boy," or "Tub-a-Lard," we stomped our feet behind Billy, chanting "Boom, Boom, Boom" as he lumbered his bulky frame down the hall. Then we came up with names like "Blubber Billy" and "Bill, Bill the Butter Boy" (and several others best left out of print). Around Thanksgiving, we droned a new line like a college fight song: "Billy, Billy is-so-hilly. Billy, Billy is-so-hilly. . . ."

Because he didn't have a beautiful older sister, a handsome face, or trendy clothes, Billy Bloom was destined to live at the very bottom of the pyramid, like medieval dirt. Lester "the toothpick" Franklin, a skinny boy with freckles and square, protruding teeth, had occupied this position since kindergarten, and he cheered up the moment Billy appeared in the doorway. In fact, Lester ended up giving Billy the hardest time of all. He got downright nasty—even put a tack on his chair one time. *That* got Lester suspended from school but elevated him to minor nobility when he returned to class and told us that his new name was "Less" and that he would only wear black clothes. He also started speaking with a raspy voice and rhyming his sentences. Suddenly, the girls thought that his thick-framed glasses and bushy eyebrows made him look older and mysterious and tough. Sixth-grade girls—go figure.

Of course I didn't know what charisma was when I was eleven years old, but I understand it now and believe that Chad Nezzar had gobs of it. He was at the top, the king, maybe even an angel, a *dark* angel, that is.

Chad wasn't particularly smart or handsome. In fact, he was kind of slow, and with his short legs, small, square head, and close-set eyes, sort of funny looking too. But that didn't matter because Chad Nezzar (or simply "Nezz," as he liked to be called) could pass a football tightly, squirt milk between his teeth, and control every boy in our class.

Nezz came to school in the latest name brands. His shoes always looked new, and in the winter, he wore expensive ski coats and told us about places like Aspen and Vail. Over spring break, he went sailing with his parents and returned with a dark tan and pictures of college girls in bikinis.

Simply put—we were amazed.

Yet, we didn't follow Nezz because of his expensive clothes or fancy vacations. It was because he had charisma and an unequaled command of the English language that we revered him. He was forceful with sentences and could forge them into daggers when he spoke. If another boy were to threaten his crown or get on his bad side, Nezz was sure to start a solid rumor about how much of a sissy that kid was or how he had seen lice in his hair. (He was equally skilled with the written word and often used the walls of the bathroom as his personal guillotine.)

As for Billy Bloom, we never really discovered much about him, only that he had to be living on the last working farm in suburban Chicago and that his parents must not have cared too much about him because they sent him to school in steel-tipped work boots and denim overalls (the kind with reinforced knees). When it was cool to wear hightop basketball shoes, parachute pants, and camouflage jackets, Billy dressed like an itinerant farmer, complete with lines of dirt under his fingernails and a lingering barnyard stink. We had Velcro and tied colorful rubber gaskets around our wrists. We proudly displayed brands like All Mine, Who's There?, and Survivor. The only writing on Billy's clothes? His own name written in capital letters across his collar. So we tormented him. We teased him incessantly, occasionally stole things out of his locker, and made a habit of tripping and pushing him in the hallway.

After Christmas break, Billy brought a rusty pocket watch to school, and things got even worse. It was connected to his belt loop by a thick chain, and every ten minutes or so, he'd open it and then inspect it like some nineteenth-century businessman, squinting one eye as if he were peering through a wire-rimmed monocle.

Billy claimed the watch belonged to his grandfather, who had taken it off a dead German gunner during World War II.

"My grandfather killed that Nazi with his bare hands," he explained on the basketball court.

But before any of us could express any interest, Nezz came up and pushed him in the chest. "That's the biggest lie I've ever heard, Blubber Face."

Billy stuttered as he insisted it was the truth and continued with a story about how his grandfather Bloom was part of a special unit called the Night Stalkers. His mission was to hunt down enemy soldiers in complete darkness, crawl into their fox holes, and snap their necks ("or slit their throats," he added casually, gesturing with his right index finger below his chin).

Without warning and with the quickness of a striking snake, Nezz reached in and snatched the old watch out of Billy's hand, causing him to whoop out loud. Then whistling an eerie tune and turning the watch over in his palm, Nezz strolled through a large group of us boys. Finally he opened it and discovered that it didn't even work.

"You're an idiot, Billy," someone yelled.

"Yeah, you're so stupid, Fatso!" began the familiar barrage of insults. And we all laughed as Nezz dropped Billy's watch onto the concrete, smiled, and put the heel of his white sneaker through the glass face.

Now, if Billy had been like Timmy Fisher or Melvin Sanchez or Pino Barchuso (who spoke broken English and lived above his family's pizzeria), he would have quietly taken up solitary games or made friends with other bottom dwellers. But he continued being Billy—brazen, loud, and fearless.

He told lie after lie, each one getting him in even deeper. First it was the one about how he had driven the pace car at the Indianapolis 500. Then came an elaborate story about his father directing movies in Los Angeles, followed by a recurring tale about sharks that he supposedly kept in an abandoned grain bin.

"You're such a liar," we would say and then tell him to shut up every time he spoke for the rest of the day.

"But, but, but . . .," he would stutter.

"No, shut up, shut up, shut up!" we'd yell back into Billy's face. And if he kept talking, we'd cover our ears and chant together, "La, la, la, la, la, la, la. We're not listening to you. La, la, la, la, la, la, la."

I don't think there was a kid in our class who wouldn't have gladly kicked Billy—repeatedly—if given the chance. He never stopped talking, not even when we ignored him. It didn't matter. He'd talk to himself, whisper bizarre stories about riding camels and unearthing rare artifacts from deep within the Amazon, stories complete with sound effects and, upon occasion, musical interludes.

And I'm fairly certain most of the teachers disliked Billy as well. He truly lied about everything. When they asked him about his missing homework, he'd stand up from his desk, push his chest out, and confidently declare that it had blown out his window or that it must have fallen from his bag on the way to school. Once, he even claimed to have used his math worksheet to bandage the leg of a horse. ("Bull**** Billy" was another name we liked to disguise in a cough or say under our breath, and I wouldn't doubt the teachers used this one in the lounge from time to time.)

In the spring, Sunnyside held its annual Kite Day. After lunch, the entire building cleared out over the schoolyard, shouting. Finally someone's kite ripped into the sky and cut back and forth above the trees.

Most of us flew brightly colored plastic kites with animated cartoon characters or action figures. We had picked them out with our mothers the day before and couldn't wait to tear into the clear cellophane packaging. Of course, Nezz had a different kind of kite. It had its own carrying case and was covered with nylon fabric. He could even control it by manipulating two wooden steering pegs that sent the brightly colored wonder into steep dives and tight barrel rolls.

And it was because so many of us were captivated by Nezz's kite that we didn't notice Billy, running as fast as his heavy legs could carry him. Once airborne, however, his kite made us stare. It was black with two piercing white eyes.

Like a swarming hive, we ran over to where Billy, breathless and sweating, struggled to maintain his balance. Between his hands, he was clutching the thickest spool of string I had ever seen.

"Where did you get that kite?" someone asked.

Wheezing a little, Billy replied, "Made it."

"Who taught you how to make a kite?"

"Built it at Scouts," was his muted response.

Now, up to this point, all of us had teased Billy about being a Boy Scout, especially on Wednesdays when he raised the flag with a corny salute. On those days we added "Goody Goody" and "Soldier Boy" to our litany of insults. But now, as we watched that amazing kite overhead, we started to have second thoughts about Scouts.

Just then, Mr. Baptista, our science teacher, approached. "How's it flying?"

Billy spoke with such excitement that his voice cracked, "Oh, Mr. B, it's flying great."

"I really like the way you decorated your kite. What do you think, guys? What do you think of Billy's eyes?"

"Cool."

"They're awesome."

"Hey, Billy, can you show me how to make a

kite like that?" someone asked.

Mr. Baptista smiled then like he knew something we didn't and patted Billy on the shoulder.

The principal always awarded ribbons for the smallest, largest, most original, and highest-flying kite. And it was clear that Billy was competing in the final category because his spool of string bulged like a melon.

"How many feet are you letting out?" someone finally asked.

Billy hesitated a moment. "Forty thousand."

There was a gasp from the crowd and then shouts, which traveled around the playground, "Billy Bloom's got forty thousand feet of string!"

"Hey, everybody, Billy's got forty thousand feet of string!"

"Couldn't that hit a plane?"

"How far is it to the moon?"

At 1:30 many students had already grounded their kites and gathered around Billy to watch the giant spool unload itself into the air. The kite was up in a steady wind and ran out with the line. Billy looked mesmerized as he watched the string bouncing back and forth between the ends of the reel, slowly shaving off layers.

By 2:00 the ribbon for smallest kite had gone to Katherine Dow, who had actually made her kite earlier that morning out of toothpicks and tissue paper. Mendon Strickler flew the largest kite, and for most original, the ribbon went to Casey Lemer whose kite revolved like a carousel and whistled like a small opening in a window.

At 2:30 Billy still had quite a bit of string left. All of the other contenders for the prize had released the extent of their line and watched their kites, which were only small dots in the sky. Occasionally, they looked over at Billy, who bit down on his lip in concentration. *His* kite was now over twenty-five thousand feet from the schoolyard, more than four and a half miles away, and racing ever farther up and out into the sky. It was less than a dot, it was a speck, a speck that many thought they saw but would squint their eyes again and claim that no it was over there farther to the east.

"No," another would say, "that's it over there."

"That's a bird," someone else would say back.

At 3:00, one of the judges, a third-grade teacher, approached the crowd with a large blue ribbon in her hand. "Well, Billy, it looks as if you've earned the ribbon for highest kite this year. Congratulations."

But Billy didn't even look up. He only nodded as he watched the line disappear off the turning spool.

No one claimed to see Billy's kite anymore, but we all imagined it tugging against the line. It was out there, somewhere, those white eyes watching down over the expressway, or staring at a passing flock of birds, or skimming past an airplane, or soaring between mountains of clouds.

"Hey, you've already won, so why don't you stop," said a small girl with glasses.

"Yeah, Billy, you're going to have to reel all of that back in you know."

But I don't think Billy heard any of this. He only held more firmly to the turning reel and licked his lips.

Almost the entire school had gathered now to watch Billy Bloom. The teachers had been talking about allowing him to let his kite out that far. They really did worry about airplanes and helicopters. But in the end, they were as fascinated as the rest of us.

It was 3:15, and the kite was *still* rising. But the end of the line was quickly approaching, so we watched Billy like a marathon runner in sight of the finish line or an explorer who spots the thinnest sliver of land. He was nearing the end and slowed the turning spool with his thumbs, witnessing the final rotations until the line stopped solidly against the triple knot tied at the base.

What followed was complete silence. The kind of silence that must come over those who make it to the peak of a mountain and gaze out over the ranges below, the awe that was certainly present when scientists detonated the first atomic bomb, or the hush that comes after hearing a secret so profound that it sucks a vacuum in your chest.

The entire school crowded around Billy, who stood in the middle and held a line that extended more than seven and a half miles. And somehow, by that thin line, we felt connected to something great. It was as if Billy opened a portal into another dimension. He held the line, his mouth parted dumbly, stepping sideways to remain balanced. However, now we didn't want to kick Billy but touch him, knowing that he was joined to that kite hanging in another world.

A school bus arrived in the circle drive, and kids started packing up their kites and going back inside. Teachers began to corral the younger children into lines.

"Good luck winding all that string, stupid" taunted Nezz, who stood with the rest of us now. "You moron, you'll be here all night."

A group of us stayed behind to watch Billy. He had forty thousand feet of string in the air, and his bus was about to leave. We didn't say anything, only envisioned those eyes so far away, the only evidence of their existence coming through the string, tugging against Billy's arms.

Nezz took a few steps out of the group and rubbed his hands together. "What are you going to do now, Billy? Your bus is leaving without you." Slowly Nezz walked up behind Billy and whispered something in his ear. Yet Billy's gaze never changed. It remained fixed, upward. Nezz said something into his other ear and poked him in the ribs—Billy only stared out as if he could actually see his kite so far from the school. Finally, Nezz spoke directly into Billy's face, "Hey, dummy, what are you going to do? You're gonna miss your bus. You're gonna miss your bus!"

At that moment Billy changed. He began to mouth words, but we couldn't understand what he was saying. Then he started to whisper and smile deeply, looking up into the sky, at a focused ray of light that came down with the string.

When this mysterious light touched Billy's hands, he didn't hesitate but tore the line from the spool in a single motion. He let it stream up into the air, toward the moon and beyond the farthest planet, through the vastness of space, until it reached the outside of everything.

THE COURSE OF EMPIRE

"Oh, I used to be so scared before they started pulsing the Midwest with brain scramblers. It wouldn't take me long to become so worked up about the changes. Believe it or not, when I was young, all of this was farm field. Now look, tract houses as far as the eye can see. And it didn't take them long once the bulldozers arrived. But I guess we knew that it was coming. The paper was complete with all of the details. The experts told us that the city just ran out of room.

Those who spoke against it held up signs that

read "WE DON'T NEED YOUR SUPER HIGHWAYS!" But the signs did little good. They came anyway and brought mega-plex movie theaters, circling news helicopters, trendy outlet malls, billboards, drive-through coffee shops, tanning salons, wholesale clubs, deluxe car washes, specialty pet shops, theme parks, . . ."

>>>>>>>>>>

"Yes, I think small towns are a safer place to live. Have I told you that already? And by the way, I agree with everything the governor said in his latest speech. We *do* need to have more warnings labels and safety classes for parents and children. He was right to point out that there are far too many sharp objects in the world. That's why I voted for him. His stance on sharp objects is going to change everything. But probably not soon enough. Just last week a woman cut her finger in the super grocery when she reached for the Sunday paper. I actually know someone who works in the deli, and she said the woman, a mother of three, was innocently humming a popular song when it happened. Luckily the bandages were just around the corner in aisle four—but think about what *could* have happened if the cut had become infected. Have you heard of this new disease that actually causes skin to glow? That's all it takes is one tiny cut, and the virus enters your bloodstream, and in no time at all, you're lit up like a firefly—permanently. Or what about all of the toxic ink in newspapers? Yeah, they say it's safe, but they also said that about florescent light bulbs. For years they sold us microwave ovens and satellite television, and look where that got us. . . ."

>>>>>>>>>>

"Where was I? That's right, I was talking about my garden. This year I'm mainly planting gourds. I haven't had much luck with tomatoes, but that isn't my fault. I hear that the clouds are changing and filtering out series B light waves. So, I'll grow some pumpkins for the neighborhood kids. Pumpkins. Is there anything more innocent than a pumpkin? Maybe a green tree leaf. But seriously, you need to visit more often. Come back in the fall when my pumpkins are ready. We can carve them and make jack-o'-lanterns for Halloween. On second thought, I don't use knives anymore and pumpkins only encourage kids to vandalize. Maybe I ought to just give up on the garden this year. I started it when I heard that produce in the new super grocery had been modified by scientists who didn't know what long-term exposure would do to the human body. Insiders say that it does some horrible things to lab rats (especially the really shiny red apples). Hey, it scared me bad enough to buy seeds and plant my own garden. The first year I had everything: green beans, tomatoes, corn, lettuce, sweet potatoes, green peppers, and even asparagus. I started to buy my bread from a man who had invented a way to remove the residual pesticide from wheat flour. Then I saw a news special on the dangers of open-air gardens and do-it-yourself seed packets and decided to scrap the whole thing. I gave up eating for an entire week before I went back to the super grocery and took my chances. . . ."

>>>>>>>>>>

"Like I was telling you before about the brain scramblers (which are technically called electromagnetic pulsators, or EPs). Wonderful invention. The ironic thing is that the government actually built them as secret weapons to fight terrorism, but now they routinely pulse all forty-seven states. I've heard that crime rates have actually dropped a little. But, more importantly, the chronic depression and waves of panic have all but disappeared in the past six years since these pulsing satellites, in fixed orbits around the earth, have taken aim at America every few minutes or so. Simply put, they shock the mind. It would be like getting slapped every so often without the pain. Sounds crude, I know, but think about it. Every few minutes, your mind goes blank. It's like having your brain wiped clean and starting from scratch, which is a little annoying when you're counting or having a conversation but indispensable in this modern world with all of its new diseases and pollutants and crime. I don't like to leave my house for fear I might get rained on or bitten by a mosquito. And last year I decided to bar up my windows and buy attack dogs. When I have to go out, I cover my entire body and speak to no one. (Never know who the kooks are. Just last week I heard an old man threatened a gas station clerk with a soft taco.) . . ."

>>>>>>>>>>

"Oh, just look at the beautiful cloud formations. I see a bunny rabbit. Do you see it? Experts say that what a person sees in a cloud can explain a lot. I had a friend who routinely saw ketchup bottles. Ah, friendship. Ketchup. Look at this. Did you know that they put lutein in ketchup? Supposed to be good for your eyes. Who would have thought? Ketchup is good for your eyes. It may contain scores of dangerous food dyes and preservatives, but it helps to promote ocular health. But it's like everything else. They say that exercise is good, but they also say that by breathing deeply, we are actually pulling more toxic air into our lungs and that it's okay to exercise as long as you only take short, quick breaths. Or, better yet, invest in a gas mask. Then you can breathe as deeply as you want. But don't wear the mask too long because the rubber liner is petroleum based, and we all know what that means. Point is there isn't a thing in the world that's completely safe. You have to drink more water, but you better know your source—and filter it through an ionized carbon block and boil it just to be safe. And I wouldn't use a straw or any imported glassware. Better just cup your hands and scoop it up the way they did years ago (only make sure that you wash first with antibacterial soap). Reading stimulates the mind, but don't touch the pages, and if you smell something musty, it could be toxic mold spores. Television is entertaining but make sure you view it reflected in a mirror. Never look directly at the screen. Americans actually did that for years. Just open any history book. . . ."

>>>>>>>>>>

"On the bright side, the brain scramblers have paid off most of the national debt. That's right. Our taxes have gone down, and for the first time since its inception, social security actually has a surplus. As a result, the government has started a new program called "Happy Days," which is designed to surprise Americans with extra money. Every week random families go to their mailboxes and find a hefty check, the government's way of saying thank you or good luck or whatever. I've gotten it a few times already. That's what I used to buy the attack dogs (they're more expensive than you think). But I suppose I ought to first explain how the brain scramblers work. Simply put, they shock the mind. It would be like getting slapped every so often without the pain. Sounds crude, I know, but think about it. Every few minutes, your mind goes blank. It's like having your brain wiped clean. You start from scratch, which is a little annoying when you're counting or having a conversation, but indispensable if you live in this modern world with its new diseases and pollution and crime. Well, after all of the success in America, other countries wanted in, so the government started to sell them pulse time, which they can now purchase on the Internet like prepaid wireless minutes. The cost is based on a sliding scale, more for big nations like Canada but reduced for small countries like Hawaii. And they keep coming back. Last I read the United States was pulsing most of Europe and Asia. For some reason Australia doesn't seem interested, but I think we're planning to pulse them now and again, so they can see what they're missing. Then I imagine we'll send them a promotional coupon in the mail or something. . . ."

>>>>>>>>>>>>

"As I was saying, I think that television news anchors are some of the friendliest people I know.

Whenever I feel overwhelmed, I turn on the news and listen to their voices. I'm not really interested in what they're talking about. I just like to see how their mouths are always smiling. It's hard to imagine a television news anchor ever doing anything to hurt you, especially the meteorologist. Yes, if I had to choose one person to be my friend it would be Chip McKinley from Channel Four. He's like a brother to me. Maybe it's his bow tie or the way he coordinates his pants and slacks with the days of the week. That's comforting to me. Chip's a really nice guy. You know I met him once. Yep, he was part of the big crowd that traveled up Route 90 to see the destruction caused by that microburst. He stood up on some of the wreckage and explained that a microburst is a strong down draft with the wind speed of a small tornado. He said that as the earth travels farther from the sun, we can expect more of them. Then he handed out some brochures, which highlighted the early warning signs and urged us to build underground houses that could withstand severe weather. What a guy. I'm telling you that he might even be president some day. I'd vote for him. I bet his policy on sharp objects and personal safety is right on. How rude of me. I didn't even offer you coffee. Do you take cream and sugar? I don't use either. Truth is that real cream is too expensive and the synthetic stuff has too many side effects. So I've gotten by drinking it black with sugar substitute. . . ."

>>>>>>>>>>

"*I* know what I wanted to tell you. It was about growing up before the pulse machines. Of course, you're too young to remember what it was like, but I'll never forget the lines of people who'd wander out onto the highways and begin walking westward. I saw it all on my television and actually have some recorded footage if you want to help me look through the attic. It all seemed so sad but strangely natural. All of a sudden some businessman leaving for work would just get out of his car, briefcase and cell phone in hand, and begin walking west, always west. And then it was like a chain reaction, tens of thousands would cluster into groups and begin the journey toward the Pacific Ocean, their arms outstretched in front of them. Psychologists called it LSC (Lost Sheep Complex), said that it was caused by overstimulation and that the only treatment was solitary confinement and television. Then there were the panic attacks triggered by used car salesmen. That's right. Don't ask me why, but they always had short names like Bill, Joe, or Stan. From what I've been told and what little I've read about the phenomenon, they would just snap and begin shouting commercials into the air. Those who studied the events said that their words actually masked subconscious suggestions that encouraged similar behavior in others. And the end result was like an outbreak of contagion, leaving entire towns running in circles promoting everything from cosmetics to fried chicken. Can you imagine, grown men clucking like chickens and then singing sales jingles about their crispy wings? Whole school buses filled with children screaming out peanut butter and diaper advertisements. Old folks like me, twirling around in circles and mimicking ads for candy bars and bottled water. Sounds like science fiction, I know, but it happened. . . ."

>>>>>>>>>>

"How rude of me. I didn't even offer you coffee. Do you take cream and sugar? I don't use either. Truth is that real cream is too expensive, and the synthetic stuff has too many side effects. So I've gotten by drinking it black with sugar substitute. Make yourself at home while I'm in the kitchen. But just don't look out that window over there, and I wouldn't sit too close to the plant in the corner. I did last week, and I haven't stopped scratching behind my ears. Not to worry though. I'm taking one of those blue pills for it. . . ."

>>>>>>>>>>

"All I had was apple drink. And I brought you some ketchup. I see that you wear glasses, and I was reading that ketchup has lutein, which is supposed to be good for your eyes. Who would have thought. Ketchup is good for your eyes. It may contain scores of dangerous food dyes and preservatives, but it helps to promote ocular health. But it's like everything else. Here, let me put a dab on your finger. Have I answered all of your questions? I know that you wanted to know about life before the pulse machines. Oh, I used to be so scared before they started pulsing the Midwest with brain scramblers. It wouldn't take me long to become so worked up about the changes. Believe it or not, when I was young, all of this was farm field. Now look, tract houses as far as the eye can see. And it didn't take them long once the bulldozers arrived. But I guess we knew that it was coming. The paper was complete with all of the details. The experts told us that the city just ran out of room.

Those who spoke against it held up signs that read "WE DON'T NEED YOUR SUPER HIGHWAYS!" But the signs did little good. They came anyway and brought mega-plex movie theaters, circling news helicopters, trendy outlet malls, billboards, drive-through coffee shops, tanning salons, wholesale clubs, deluxe car washes, specialty pet shops, theme parks, . . ."

>>>>>>>>>>

>>>>>>>>>>

>>>>>>>>>>

>>>>>>>>>>

>>>>>>>>>>

>>>>>>>>>>

>>>>>>>>>>

>>>>>>>>>>

>>>>>>>>>>

>>>>>>>>>>

>>>>>>>>>>

About the Author

John Napolitano teaches writing in West Central Illinois. *American Floaters* is his first book.